LITTLE PRINCESS

Written and Illustrated by Chetty D.

Visit www.fb.me/authorchettyd for new releases!

Little Vivy was a princess, Daddy always said.

But how could Vivy be a princess with no crown on her head?

She didn't own a tiara, just some funny hats.

She wasn't guarded
by a dragon, but
by a lazy cat.

She didn't have a giant castle, just a tiny house.

She didn't sing to woodland creatures, not even to her mouse.

She didn't own a hundred gowns, just a fancy dress.

She had no maids to clean her room, at times it was a mess.

It isn't that she minded this, but she just had to know.

If Vivy truly was a princess, how come it didn't show?

Daddy swore she was a princess, lying would be mean.

Daddy proved she was a princess, by treating Mommy like a queen.

Made in the USA
Middletown, DE
28 December 2023

46914988R00015